Bye Bye Binky

Written by
M.S. Johnson

Illustrated by
David Ampudia
Martinez

DEDICATED

To my daughter MADISON,
who has always shown me that
I can get through anything, no
matter how big or small.

Oh Binky!
Oh Binky!
What shall I do?
How am I to
sleep on my own,
without you?

You have been there, since mommy gave me life. You were there my first morning, as well as my first night.

When I was fussy, you helped calm me down.

You were my
best friend.
I thought you'd
always be around.

But my mommy says
I'm big now,
even though I feel
so *scared*.

I miss being little,
when I didn't have
a *care*.

Oh, mommy give me blankets, or maybe a new bear... something to help me cope with all of my big fears!

To you, it was
a binky,
but it was more than
that to me.
With it by my side,
there was much that
I could be.

Bye Bye

Binky!

We have had many *fun* times.

Deep down in my *heart,* you will always be mine.

Made in the USA
Las Vegas, NV
25 January 2024